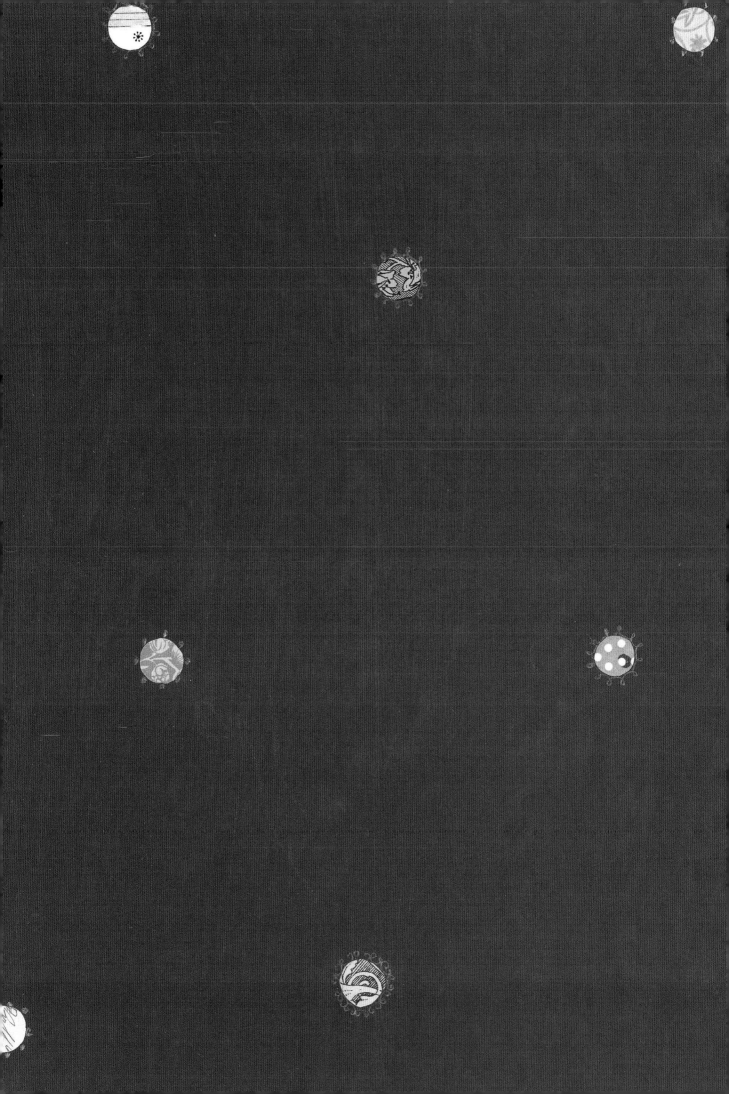

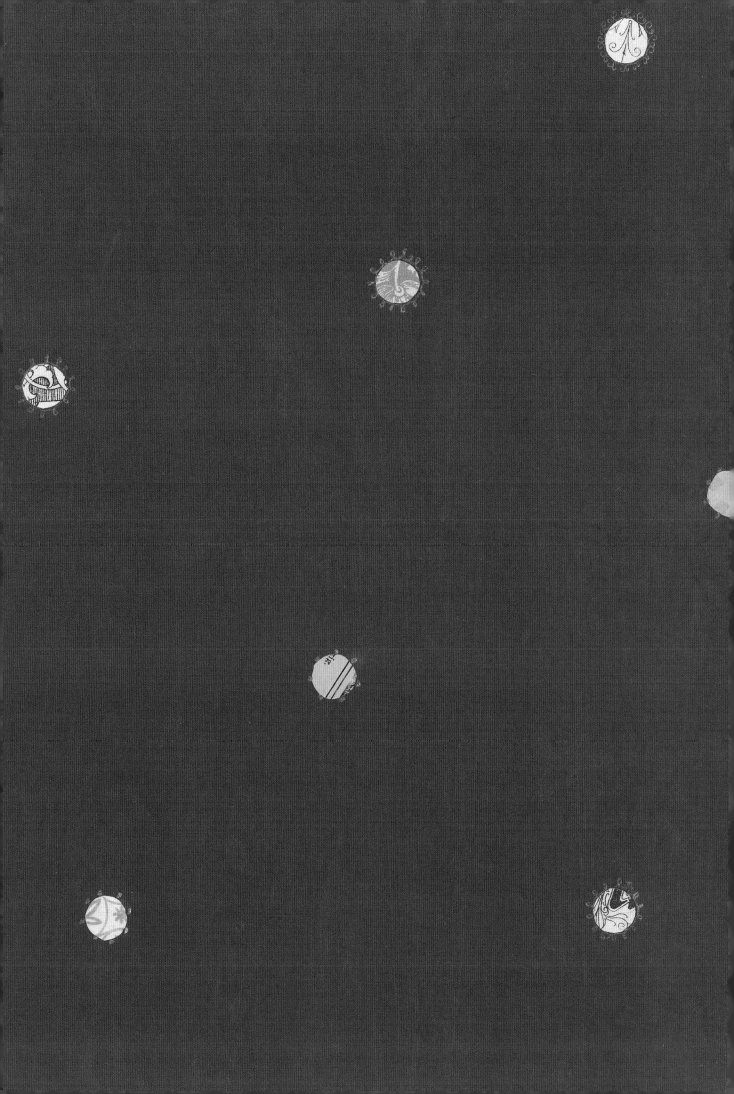

For Leonhardt & Ferdinand

First published in the United States, Great Britain, Canada, Australia, and New Zealand in 2009
by North-South Books Inc.,
an imprint of NordSüd Verlag AG, CH-8005 Zürich, Switzerland.
First paperback edition published in 2012 by North-South Book Inc.
Distributed in the United States by North-South Books Inc., New York 10016.

Library of Congress Cataloging-in-Publication Data is available.
ISBN: 978-0-7358-2235-1 (trade edition).
4 6 8 10 9 9 7 5 3
ISBN: 978-0-7358-4094-2 (paperback edition)
2 4 6 8 10 9 9 7 5 3 1
Printed in China by Leo Paper Products Ltd., Heshan, Guangdong, June 2012

www.northsouth.com

"I Have a
Little Problem,"
said the bear

by Heinz Janisch

illustrated by Silke Leffler

NorthSouth
New York / London

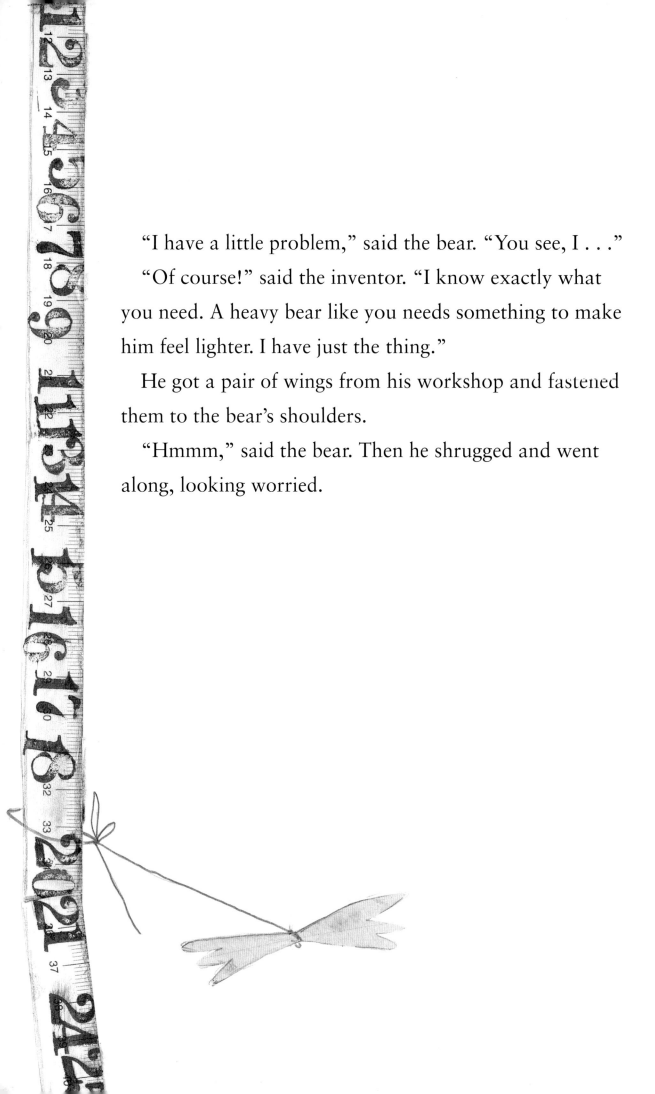

"I have a little problem," said the bear. "You see, I . . ."

"Of course!" said the inventor. "I know exactly what you need. A heavy bear like you needs something to make him feel lighter. I have just the thing."

He got a pair of wings from his workshop and fastened them to the bear's shoulders.

"Hmmm," said the bear. Then he shrugged and went along, looking worried.

"I have a little problem," said the bear. "You see . . ."

"Indeed I do," said the tailor. "Your wings are very handsome, but you need a scarf." And he wound a long scarf around the bear's neck.

"Hmmm," said the bear. Then he shrugged and went along, looking worried.

"I have a little problem," said the bear.
"You . . ."

"I'm just the man you're looking for!"
said the hatter. "Now don't say a word.
I have just the thing for you." And he
placed a fine hat on the bear's head.

"Hmmm," said the bear. Then he
shrugged and went along, looking worried.

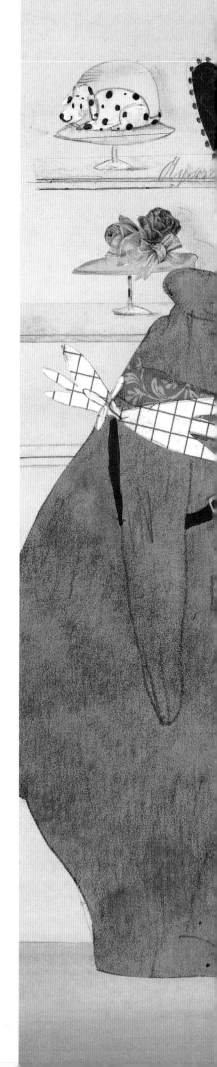

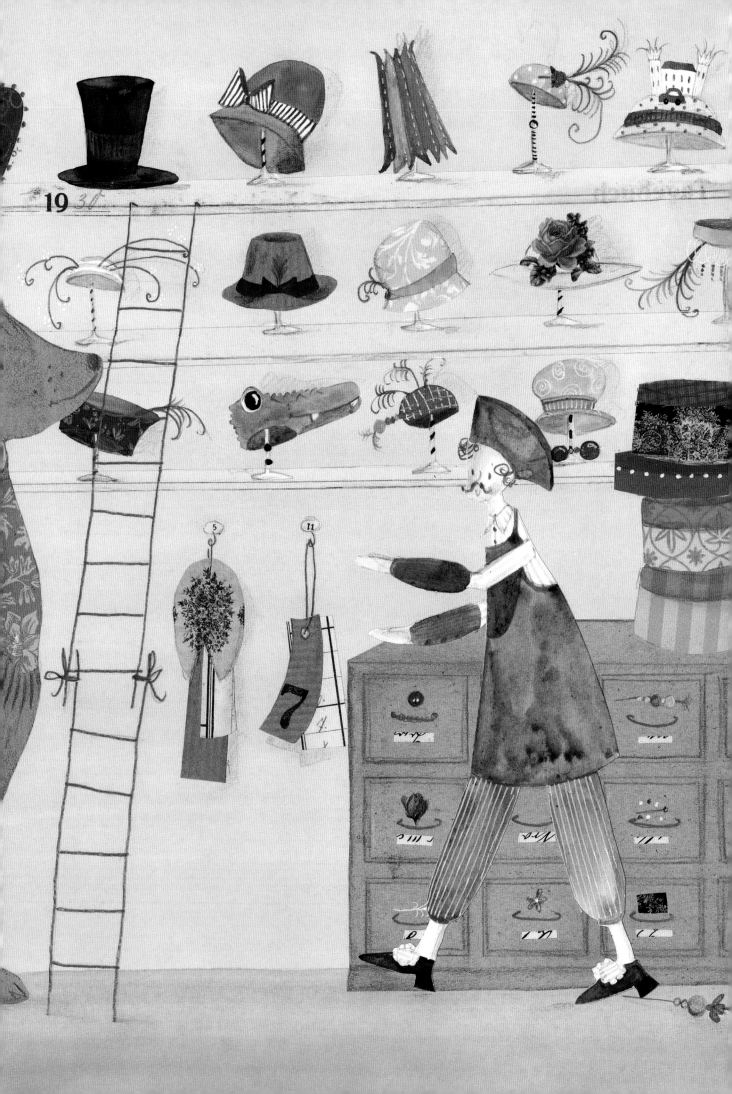

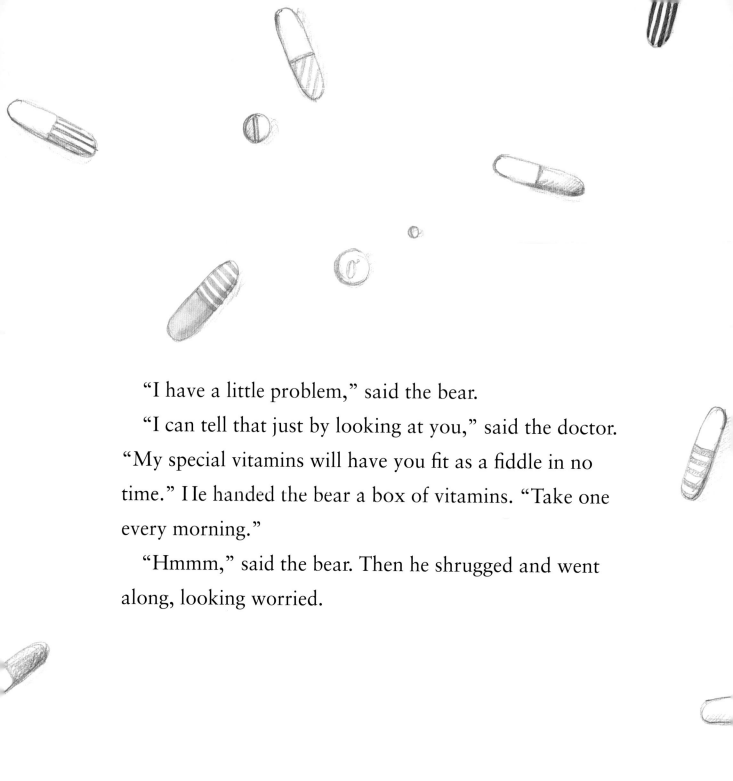

"I have a little problem," said the bear.

"I can tell that just by looking at you," said the doctor. "My special vitamins will have you fit as a fiddle in no time." He handed the bear a box of vitamins. "Take one every morning."

"Hmmm," said the bear. Then he shrugged and went along, looking worried.

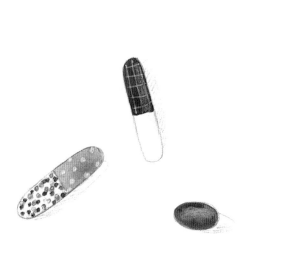

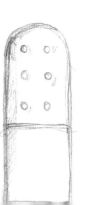

"I have a little . . ." said the bear.

"Problem!" said the street vendor. "But I have the cure! This little charm will bring you good luck wherever you go." And he hung a silver pig on a chain around the bear's neck.

"Hmmm," said the bear. Then he shrugged and went along, looking worried.

"I have a . . ." said the bear.

"Well I can see you have a problem," said the eye doctor. "That's why I'm here." She placed a pair of glasses on the bear's nose. "Now, isn't that better?"

"Hmmm," said the bear. Then he shrugged and went along, looking worried.

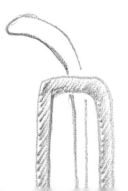

"I have . . ." said the bear.

"A little problem?" said the shopkeeper. "Well, never you worry, my dear. This honey will sweeten up your life in no time." And she handed the bear a jar of honey.

"Hmmm," said the bear. Then he shrugged and went along, looking worried.

"I . . ." said the bear

"*YOU* have a problem," said the shoemaker. "You need boots!" She pulled a pair of boots from a box. "A real bear needs real bear boots," she said, "and these are the best bear boots I have. A perfect fit!"

"Hmmm," said the bear. Then he shrugged and went along, looking worried.

At the top of a hill, the bear stopped.
He looked back over the town and shook
his head. He was worn out.

The bear unfastened his wings. He took off his hat
and scarf. He took off his glasses and the pig on a chain.
He kicked off his boots. He set his vitamins and honey
on the ground. Then he sat down on the hill and sighed.

"What's the matter?" asked a fly on a blade of grass beside him.

"I don't want to talk about it," said the bear. "No one listens to me anyway."

"I'm listening," said the fly. "Tell me about it."

"I have a little problem," said the bear. "You see, I'm afraid of the dark, alone in my cave. There are no other bears for miles around, and I don't know anyone who wants to sleep in my cave with me. I dread the darkness all day long."

"That really is a problem," said the fly. "But I have a solution. It just so happens that I am looking for somewhere to live. A bear's cave sounds very cozy. I could move in with you. What do you say?"

"Hmmm," said the Bear. "I feel better already."

So the fly hopped onto the Bear's shoulder, where she made herself comfortable.

Then off they went together, looking happy.